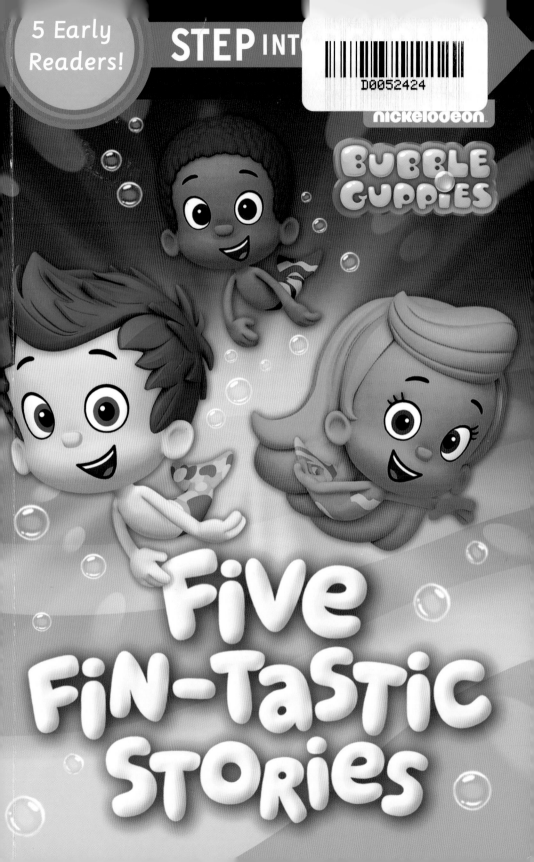

STEP INTO

D0052424

nickelodeon

BUBBLE GUPPIES

Five FiN-TasTiC sToRiEs

Dear Parent:

Congratulations! Your child is taking the first steps on an exciting journey. The destination? Independent reading!

STEP INTO READING® will help your child get there. The program offers five steps to reading success. Each step includes fun stories and colorful art. There are also Step into Reading Sticker Books, Step into Reading Math Readers, Step into Reading Phonics Readers, Step into Reading Write-In Readers, and Step into Reading Phonics Boxed Sets—a complete literacy program with something for every child.

Learning to Read, Step by Step!

Ready to Read Preschool–Kindergarten
• big type and easy words • rhyme and rhythm • picture clues
For children who know the alphabet and are eager to begin reading.

Reading with Help Preschool–Grade 1
• basic vocabulary • short sentences • simple stories
For children who recognize familiar words and sound out new words with help.

Reading on Your Own Grades 1–3
• engaging characters • easy-to-follow plots • popular topics
For children who are ready to read on their own.

Reading Paragraphs Grades 2–3
• challenging vocabulary • short paragraphs • exciting stories
For newly independent readers who read simple sentences with confidence.

Ready for Chapters Grades 2–4
• chapters • longer paragraphs • full-color art
For children who want to take the plunge into chapter books but still like colorful pictures.

STEP INTO READING® is designed to give every child a successful reading experience. The grade levels are only guides. Children can progress through the steps at their own speed, developing confidence in their reading, no matter what their grade.

Remember, a lifetime love of reading starts with a single step!

Five Fin-Tastic Stories

Step into Reading, Random House, and the Random House colophon are registered trademarks of Random House LLC.

Visit us on the Web!
StepIntoReading.com
randomhousekids.com

Educators and librarians, for a variety of teaching tools, visit us at RHTeachersLibrarians.com

ISBN 978-0-553-52116-0

MANUFACTURED IN CHINA

10 9 8 7 6 5 4 3 2 1

STEP INTO READING®

nickelodeon

BUBBLE GUPPIES™

Five Fin-Tastic Stories

Step 1 and Step 2 Books
A Collection of Five
Early Readers

Random House 🏠 New York

Contents

BUBBLE GUPPIES™

THE BEST DOGHOUSE EVER!

We love Bubble Puppy!

He is a great pet.

Bubble Puppy needs
a doghouse.
We ask our friends
for help.

The crabs draw a plan.

It is a doghouse.

17

We get wood and nails.

Nails

18

We get paint and tools, too.

We put on
our hard hats.

The hats

keep us safe.

It is time to start.

We check

the house plan.

Zip, zip, zip!

A crab saws wood.

Bang, bang, bang!

We hammer the nails.

Twist, twist, twist!
A crab turns
the screw.

Crank, crank, crank!

A crab turns the wrench.

The house is done!
We show Bubble Puppy.

Bubble Puppy

toots the horn.

He loves

his new doghouse.

All right!
We built
the best doghouse ever!

BUBBLE GUPPIES

BIG TRUCK SHOW!

Honk, honk!

Beep, beep!

Here come

the trucks!

A fire truck is red.

It has a ladder.

The siren flashes.

The siren is loud!

A dump truck
is full of sand.
The back goes up.
The sand slides out!

41

A garbage truck
takes trash away.
Pee-yew!

Gil and Molly
hold their noses!

A mail truck
brings mail.

Goby gets a letter!

Jingle, jingle!
Here comes
the ice cream truck!

Deema eats
a sweet treat.

Oona and Nonny
drive a bread truck.

The bread truck
will soon be back
and on a roll!

It is time
for the big truck show!

The crowd
claps and cheers.

There are big trucks.

There are little trucks.

They are very
helpful trucks!

Humunga-Truck

comes out.

It is really big!

Uh-oh!
The big truck
is stuck
in the mud!

Zoom, zoom!
Here comes
the tow truck!

The tow truck
hooks the big truck.

It pulls the big truck
out of the mud!

Hooray for trucks!
Hooray for
Humunga-Truck!

THE SPRING CHICKEN!

Spring is in the air!
A bird chirps.

A butterfly
beats its wings.

Tadpoles swim
in the pond.

We fly a kite.

71

It is picnic time!

We eat outside.

The warm sun
shines down.

The Spring Chicken
comes today!
We decorate
the stage.
The mayor helps.

The mayor gives
Oona a plant.
She will help it grow.

We water the plant.

We give the plant
plenty of sun.

The Spring Chicken
is here!
He will say
it is spring
when he sees
a flower bloom!

Oona's plant blooms
into a flower.

The Spring Chicken
sees the flower.
That means
it is spring!
We clap and cheer.

We flap our wings.

"Bawk, bawk, bawk!"

We do
the Spring Chicken dance!

Happy spring!

Howdy!
Look.
Cowgirl Dusty
rides into town.

She rides
her horse, Rusty.
Giddy-up!

Cowgirl Dusty ropes
a young calf
with her lasso.

A lasso is
a loop of rope.
Cowboys and cowgirls
twirl lassos.

Molly wants
to be a cowgirl.
She wears
a cowgirl hat.

She puts on
a cowgirl vest.

She rides

a horse.

She does tricks
with her lasso!

It is fun to be

a cowboy

or a cowgirl!

Molly and her friends
twirl their lassos.
They do
a lasso dance!

The cowgirl parade
is today.

The sun is shining.

Balloons float.

It is a party!

Yee-haw!

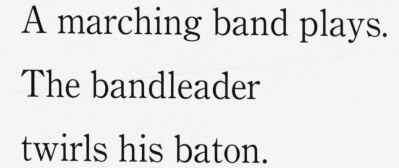

A marching band plays.
The bandleader
twirls his baton.

Music fills the air.

Everyone dances!

Cowgirls ride in
on their horses.
They wave flags.

The crowd claps
and cheers.

Cows follow

the cowgirls.

Look!
A baby calf.
Moo!

Cowgirl Dusty
rides in on Rusty.
She twirls her lasso.

A balloon pops.

BANG!

The sound scares
the calf.

Oh, no!
The calf
runs away!
Who will
catch the calf?

Molly knows
what to do.

She climbs
onto Rusty.
Giddy-up!

Molly twirls
her lasso
like a real cowgirl.

She ropes

the calf!

The crowd roars!
Molly is the hero
of the cowgirl parade!

Yee-haw!
Giddy-up, Guppies!

STEP **2**
READING WITH HELP

STEP INTO READING®

BUBBLE GUPPIES

THE BIG MAGIC SHOW!

124

Look!

The Amazing Daisy

has come to town.

She is

a magician.

Daisy does
a magic trick.
Molly and Gil
get to help!
Daisy climbs into a box.

Gil waves

a magic wand.

Molly says

a magic word.

Poof!

Daisy is gone!

Gil looks left.

Molly looks right.

Where did Daisy go?

Daisy is
behind the tree!
How did
she get there?

Daisy climbed
out of the box.

What a good

magic trick!

Molly wants
to do magic
just like Daisy.
What does she need?

Molly needs
a magic wand.

She needs
a magic hat.

Molly needs to say
the magic word.

Magic is not easy.

It takes practice.

The big magic show
is tonight!

The lights are bright.

The crowd cheers.

Molly brings
an elephant onstage.
She needs to make
the elephant disappear.

Molly waves a wand.
She says
the magic word.

Gil will press
a button.

The elephant will go
into the secret door.
Poof!

Molly has an idea.

There is

a secret door

in the floor.

It is a big trick.

Can Molly do it?